# The Midnight Ride of
# Flat Revere

# CATCH ALL OF FLAT STANLEY'S WORLDWIDE ADVENTURES!

The Mount Rushmore Calamity

The Great Egyptian Grave Robbery

The Japanese Ninja Surprise

The Intrepid Canadian Expedition

The Amazing Mexican Secret

The African Safari Discovery

The Flying Chinese Wonders

The Australian Boomerang Bonanza

The US Capital Commotion

Showdown at the Alamo

Framed in France

Escape to California

# AND DON'T MISS ANY OF THESE OUTRAGEOUS STORIES!

Flat Stanley: His Original Adventure!

Stanley and the Magic Lamp

Invisible Stanley

Stanley's Christmas Adventure

Stanley in Space

Stanley, Flat Again!

FLAT STANLEY's
WORLDWIDE ADVENTURES 13
BOOK No.

# The Midnight Ride of
# Flat Revere

CREATED BY **Jeff Brown**
WRITTEN BY Kate Egan
PICTURES BY Macky Pamintuan

**HARPER**
*An Imprint of HarperCollinsPublishers*

Flat Stanley's Worldwide Adventures #13: The Midnight Ride of Flat Revere
Text copyright © 2016 by the Trust u/w/o Richard C. Brown f/b/o Duncan Brown.
Illustrations by Macky Pamintuan, copyright © 2016 by HarperCollins Publishers.
All rights reserved. Printed in the United States of America.
No part of this book may be used or reproduced in any manner whatsoever without
written permission except in the case of brief quotations embodied in critical articles
and reviews. For information address HarperCollins Children's Books, a division of
HarperCollins Publishers, 195 Broadway, New York, NY 10007.
www.harpercollinschildrens.com

Library of Congress Control Number: 2016938988
ISBN 978-0-06-236604-7 (trade bdg.) — ISBN 978-0-06-236603-0 (pbk.)

Typography by Alison Klapthor
16  17  18  19  20    OPM    10  9  8  7  6  5  4  3  2  1
❖
First Edit
Also ava

# CONTENTS

# Duck Tour!

Ever since a bulletin board had fallen off the wall beside his bed—and made him as flat as a pancake—Stanley Lambchop had traveled all around the world. Sometimes he went on secret missions—as the world's most famous flat person, there were some problems that only *he* could solve. And sometimes he went on vacation, just for fun. But even though Stanley had been on almost every continent—and visited many famous places—he had never, not once, been on a duck tour.

Actually, he didn't even know what a duck tour was! But he was about to find out.

The Lambchops were visiting Boston for a long weekend getaway, and Boston, his mother told him, was famous for its duck tours. "This is the best way for us to get an overview of the whole city," Mrs. Lambchop said as they hurried to get in line. "Once we see the whole city, then we can decide what else to do while we are here."

That made sense to Stanley. The only problem was that his father and his younger brother, Arthur, already knew what they wanted to do . . . and it was not a duck tour at all.

Mr. Lambchop wanted to see Boston's historic sites. "Boston is one of America's oldest cities," Mr. Lambchop told his sons. "It started as a town in the British colony of Massachusetts. Then, in the 1700s, some colonists took the first steps toward freeing our country from British rule. Without our Revolutionary War, we would not have the country that we live in today!"

"And we would not have the

aquarium, or the science museum, or the Boston Red Sox either!" said Arthur. "Those are the things that *I* really want to see on this trip." Arthur was more interested in new Boston than in old Boston. And he was a lot more excited about sports than history.

Stanley walked ahead of them a little. He wasn't sure what he wanted to do in Boston. He only knew what he *didn't* want to do. Something was bothering him. Right now he didn't even want to think about it.

Stanley was the first to hand over his ticket and board the strangest vehicle he had ever seen. It looked a little like a boat, but it had wheels. With a flat

top and rows of seats inside, it also reminded Stanley of a school bus. If a school bus had rainbow stripes!

"I don't know why they call it a duck," said Stanley to Arthur, who was walking up behind him. "It doesn't look like a duck at all."

Mrs. Lambchop pointed at the words on its side. "Look!" she said. "Its name is Fenway Franny!"

"Maybe it will take us to the game," said Arthur. "Fenway Park is where the Red Sox play baseball."

Just then, a woman in a lighthouse T-shirt walked off the boat to greet everyone. "Hello, visitors of Boston! I'm Beacon Jill," she said, "and I'll be

your con-*duck*-tor today. I will show you all the city's highlights!" She directed them to sit inside the strange vehicle.

"You folks can squeeze in right here," said Beacon Jill to another family. She pointed to a spot next to Stanley. Being flat, he didn't take up much room at all.

Two adults sat down with a tiny girl. "I know you," she announced, her pigtails bouncing. "You're Flat Stanley!"

"Shhh, Zoey," said her dad. "Don't bother the boy."

But Stanley just smiled. He was used to being recognized wherever he went. "Yes," he said politely. "It's nice to meet you."

The vehicle was moving now, and Beacon Jill was beginning her tour. "A duck tour is the best way to get to know the city of Boston," she said into a microphone. Mrs. Lambchop nodded in agreement. "This vehicle is modeled after some amphibious trucks called DUKWs—or ducks—used during World War Two."

"Amphibious?" Arthur whispered to Stanley. "What's that?"

Stanley shrugged. He didn't know, but he could guess. "Like an amphibian, maybe?" he said. Amphibians were creatures like frogs, which start their lives in the water but eventually move to land.

Arthur shook his head. "That can't be it," he said. "Ducks are birds."

They drove through the city, past a giant library and a glass skyscraper called the John Hancock Tower, which was one of Boston's tallest buildings. Then they turned into a big green park. "Here in the Boston Public Garden, there are some statues that I think the children would like to see," said Beacon Jill. "Follow me, and don't forget your cameras!" The whole tour group climbed out for a stroll.

Right on the edge of a path, there was a statue of a mother duck. Eight little duckling statues trailed behind her. "Does anyone know what these are?"

Beacon Jill asked the group.

Zoey called out, "*Make Way for Ducklings*!" Stanley remembered that was the title of a book he loved when he was little. It was about the Mallard family, looking for a place in Boston to raise their babies. Now he saw that it took place right here in the Public Garden!

"*That* must be why it's called a duck tour," Arthur said.

Back on the truck, Beacon Jill pointed out the gold-domed State House, in the middle of an old neighborhood called Beacon Hill, and Stanley figured out how she got her name. She also told the group when they were entering the city's North End, which was famous for its Italian restaurants. There is certainly a lot to see in Boston! Stanley thought.

They passed a long brick building perched above a river. "Look, it's the science museum!" Arthur told Mrs. Lambchop. "Let's go there as soon as this tour is over."

Before his mother could answer,

Beacon Jill yelled out, "Okay now, get ready for . . . splashdown!"

All of a sudden, the truck drove right up to the edge of the water—and plunged right in!

It wasn't a truck anymore—it was a boat!

Mr. Lambchop wiped his face dry and said, "I think *this* is why it's called a duck tour."

"And an amphibious vehicle," Stanley added. Like an amphibian, it could go on land *and* water.

"Welcome to the Charles River," said Beacon Jill. Stanley and the others looked around. The river was lined with trees and dotted with boats. The duck boat sailed under a stone bridge, and it seemed like they were in a whole different city now. There were no traffic jams on the river, and the John Hancock Tower seemed far away. "Breathe in the salt air, boys," said Mrs. Lambchop. "We're not too far from the ocean!" A seagull soared on the breeze.

The tour stopped for a little while, as Beacon Jill answered some questions. Mr. Lambchop pointed to some buildings on the other side of the river. "There's Cambridge, home to some of the country's best universities," he told Stanley. "That's where the doctors'

conference is. That's where you'll be speaking, Stanley!"

*That* was the thing that Stanley didn't want to think about.

On this trip, the Lambchops would be meeting up with one of their good friends from home—Dr. Dan, who was visiting Boston at the same time as they were!

Normally, Stanley loved to see Dr. Dan. He was the nicest doctor ever! But Stanley was nervous about seeing him here.

Dr. Dan was in Boston to talk to a group of doctors about an exciting new scientific discovery. New research had shown him different ways to help people who wanted to lose weight, people who wanted to gain weight, or other people who wanted to change their size or shape . . . even people who were flat!

In a big speech at the end of the conference, Dr. Dan would tell the other doctors what he had learned

and what it could mean. He had also invited Stanley to give a speech of his own. "This discovery could help you, Stanley!" Dr. Dan had said. "One of these days, we'll be able to get you back to normal. Will you tell the doctors how that would change your life?"

Stanley didn't want to give a speech in the middle of his family vacation. And he felt pretty normal already. He had made a huge mistake, though. When Dr. Dan asked him to speak, Stanley had not exactly said *no*. Dr. Dan was his friend, and Stanley didn't know how to tell him the truth.

In Boston, then, Stanley would have to do one of two hard things. He could disappoint Dr. Dan at the last minute, which would be terrible. Or he could make a big speech to a group of strangers, which might be worse.

And he didn't know which one he would do. Was there a way to avoid either of these bad choices?

# Rubber Ducky Rescue

Beacon Jill started the boat again, and asked for a volunteer driver. Zoey jumped up and drove for a few minutes, and then came back to her seat with a rubber ducky souvenir. She was all smiles as Beacon Jill started speaking. "If you look right there," she said, pointing to something in the distance, "you can see the very top of the Old

North Church. When British soldiers arrived in Boston in 1775, Paul Revere put signals there to warn the colonists. The very next day, the Revolutionary War broke out!"

Mr. Lambchop's eyes lit up. He raised his hand to ask a question. "Is the Old North Church a part of the Freedom Trail?"

Beacon Jill nodded. "The Freedom Trail is a pathway that connects all of Boston's important historic sites," she explained. "You can walk easily from one to the other."

"Sounds like the perfect way to start exploring Boston's history," Mr. Lambchop said.

Arthur didn't look very happy. "What about the science museum?" he complained. "When can we do what I want to do?"

Mr. Lambchop sighed, too. "Everyone

will get to do what they want to do in Boston, Arthur," he said. "You just need to be patient."

"The Freedom Trail is wonderful," Beacon Jill told Arthur. "You'll learn how the colonists fought for freedom. They wanted to be able to make the rules for themselves!"

"I know just how they felt," Arthur grumbled. "I would like to be in charge for once!" Before anyone could reply, Zoey shrieked. "No! My ducky!"

One minute, the rubber ducky was in Zoey's hands. The next minute, he was floating in the Charles River.

Zoey started to cry. "I just came up with a name for him," she said through her tears. "I was going to call him Lucky." He bounced along on the little waves made by a passing sailboat.

A man in a blue kayak called up to her. "Is that your duck?" he said.

Zoey's dad yelled back, "Yes! Can you get him?"

The kayaker stuck the paddle way out of his boat. But when he tried to scoop up the ducky, he only dropped him back into the water. Lucky got up a little burst of speed, and it looked like he was swimming away.

Zoey covered her eyes with her hands. Her shoulders were shaking, even when her mom put her arm around her. "It's okay," she said. "We'll find a way to get him."

"What if I try to get a little closer?" Beacon Jill said, helpfully.

"Yes, please. Whatever you can do to bring back Lucky," Zoey cried.

"Zoey has such nice manners," whispered Mrs. Lambchop. "I hope she can get Lucky back."

But moving the tour duck only made the rubber duck float off in the other direction. And even if they got right next to the ducky, nobody could reach into the river.

Well, nobody except Flat Stanley. He didn't know anything about giving a speech at a medical conference. But he did know how to help out in an emergency.

All he had to do was look at his brother. They had a whole conversation with their eyes. "We can do it!" Arthur's look said.

"I think we can help," Stanley told Beacon Jill. "We can be the lifeguards for Lucky!"

"I can't let you dive in," said Beacon Jill. "I'm sorry, but swimming is not allowed on the duck tour."

Zoey let out another sob.

"I don't need to go swimming,"

Stanley explained. "All you need to do is lower me into the water."

"Sorry. There is a rule against that, too," said Beacon Jill. "We can't use the life preservers for any reason other than saving lives.

"We will be saving Lucky's life," Arthur pointed out.

Stanley wasn't sure if that counted. He said, "You don't even need to use the life preservers. I'm so flat that I can *be* a life preserver!" He stretched his body into an O for a minute, just to show her the possibilities. "I'll be able to reach Lucky. All we need is a rope for you to keep me connected. Are there any rules against that?"

"I don't think that anyone has thought up that rule yet." Beacon Jill smiled. "I'm the captain today, and I say it's okay for us to try!"

She glanced at Mr. and Mrs. Lambchop for permission, and they both nodded.

Beacon Jill went to a storage area near her steering wheel. Inside, there were brooms and trash bags and a couple of lengths of rope. "How's this?" she said, handing one to Stanley.

"Hurry!" said Zoey. "Look!" A powerboat was zipping down the river, heading toward Lucky!

Quickly, Arthur wrapped the rope around Stanley's waist like a belt.

He stood on the edge of the duck boat. "One, two, three!" said Arthur, as he picked up Stanley and threw him into the Charles River, just a few feet away from Lucky.

Stanley landed with a light splash.

The water was cold and murky. He couldn't see anything underneath him. The water was moving a lot, because it was such a busy river. This was definitely a part of Boston he hadn't expected to see!

Carefully, Stanley stretched out on the surface of the water. Any motion could send the ducky in the wrong direction. Floating was easy for Stanley, but steering was tricky.

Lucky was still bobbing happily in the water. He did not seem to mind being the smallest craft on the river. Every once in a while, a wave splashed over him. He changed course, but he never went under. And Stanley didn't

let Lucky out of his sight.

The powerboat would pass very soon. It wasn't on track to hit Lucky, but it left a long trail of water behind it, and the ripple could send Lucky farther than the rope would reach.

With only a little shaking, Stanley made a ripple in the water himself! Suddenly he saw he could use that to his advantage. When Stanley's ripple reached Lucky, the ducky popped out of the water a little. Lucky flew through the air and landed right in the middle of the Stanley life preserver!

"I've got him!" Stanley called.

Arthur yanked the rope and handed a length of it to Beacon Jill. Then he yanked again and again until Stanley was right at the edge of the boat. He climbed the last section of rope with Lucky in his hand, until he was back on board, dripping wet. Mrs. Lambchop wrapped him in a blanket.

Zoey flung her arms around him. "Thank you, Flat Stanley!" she said.

Her mom shook Stanley's hand over and over.

For some reason, the hand-shaking reminded Stanley of the doctors. He'd probably have to shake hands at the conference, too. Everyone would want to meet him and greet him because he was famously flat.

But then he would talk about *not* being flat, Stanley realized. That's what Dr. Dan meant by getting back to normal. New advances in science could make Stanley just like everyone else. Just the way he used to be.

But that wasn't normal for Stanley anymore. He didn't want to do that at all! He was used to being flat. He liked all the special things it allowed him to do, like diving into the Charles River and helping a sad little girl. He wanted to stay just the way he was.

Stanley sighed. Somehow, he was going to have to be honest with Dr. Dan.

# Quincy Market

The Lambchop family didn't see Dr. Dan until the next day, when they planned to meet for lunch at a place called Quincy Market. Settling on what to eat was as hard as deciding what to see in Boston!

Quincy Market was not one restaurant. It was many restaurants, all at once! There was a long hallway lined

with booths. Each booth had a different kind of food, like pizza or hamburgers or tacos. Stanley wondered what was in the tacos. When he was in Mexico, he had discovered a secret ingredient that made all tacos *muy bueno*! Now that he thought about it, if he wasn't flat, he wouldn't have been able to mail himself there or track it down.

Arthur pointed to two booths. "I think we should go here and here," he said.

Mrs. Lambchop frowned. "Arthur, cupcakes and ice cream do not make a well-balanced meal!" she said. She was a big believer in good nutrition.

Arthur groaned, but he and Stanley

got sandwiches and lemonades instead.
They carried their trays into a big room
full of tables and chairs. It was much
more crowded than the lunchroom
at school.

"Over here!" called Dr.
Dan, waving. He was at

a large round table. Now Stanley knew why he had not noticed him sooner. Dr. Dan was in his regular clothes, not his white doctor coat. Here in Boston, he looked just like everybody else!

"How wonderful to see the Lambchop family!" Dr. Dan said as they all sat down. "Have you had a good trip so far? I've seen the whole city from the top of the Hancock Tower!"

Arthur told him about their adventure on the duck tour.

"And how is the conference?" Mrs. Lambchop asked their friend.

Dr. Dan looked over his glasses. "Very interesting," he said. "I have met doctors from all over the world."

He looked right at Stanley. "One of them, Dr. Deb, can't wait to meet you."

"Oh," said Stanley. He put down his sandwich. Suddenly, he wasn't hungry anymore.

Dr. Dan continued. "Dr. Deb is very nice," he said, "and she knows more than anyone in the world about flatness. She will be helping me take my research to the next level."

Stanley frowned. If anyone is an expert on flatness, Stanley thought, it is me!

It was time to talk to Dr. Dan.

"Dr. Deb sounds really smart, but . . . ," he began.

He searched for the words to explain everything else. He just wanted to have fun on his trip! He didn't want people looking at him or trying to cure him. He was happy just the way he was!

But before he could get the words out of his mouth, his father changed the subject.

"Have you seen the rest of this place?" he asked Dr. Dan. "It's amazing! Did you know . . ."

Mr. Lambchop was really excited about the history in and around Quincy Market, and he recited some fun facts to Dr. Dan and the rest of the family.

His enthusiasm swept everything else away. In no time, he was clearing the table and leading the rest of them away to see the sights. Stanley didn't have a chance to speak up!

It turned out that Quincy Market was part of a bigger market called Faneuil Hall. "Long ago, this was where colonists could buy and sell things they needed. Almost like a grocery store," Mr. Lambchop said. "It was also a place where the people of Boston gathered to complain about the king."

Even Arthur was amazed. He squinted at an ice cream stand. "Right here?" he said. "That's unbelievable!"

"Well, not exactly *here*," said Mr.

Lambchop. "In a different building nearby. Follow me!"

Mr. Lambchop led them out of Quincy Market and into a wide-open space that was also full of people. These people weren't eating, though. They were watching a juggler!

He juggled five beanbags. Then he juggled five basketballs. Then he juggled upside down! Stanley could have watched him all day. And there were other street performers, too. Stanley counted as one acrobat did thirty flips in a row. It was like a circus out here! He had a feeling that this place looked different in colonial times.

Dr. Dan was chatting with Mr. and

Mrs. Lambchop. Just one more minute, Stanley thought. Then I will be brave enough to try again and tell Dr. Dan how I feel.

When Stanley looked away from the juggler, he saw a row of pushcarts selling

everything from hats and sunglasses to dog treats! It was still a marketplace, but these days it sold different things.

Arthur tapped his shoulder. "Look what I bought!" he said, holding up a pair of red socks! "You know, like the Red Sox?" Arthur said.

"Wicked cool!" said Stanley. Beacon Jill had told him that was a real compliment in Boston.

Mr. Lambchop pointed at a brick building. "That's the original Faneuil Hall," he told the boys. "Sometimes people call it the 'Cradle of Liberty.'"

"The place where liberty was a baby?" asked Arthur.

Mr. Lambchop smiled. "The place

where the people of Boston started talking about breaking away from England," he explained. "Many gave speeches at Faneuil Hall. Later, those people wrote and signed the Declaration of Independence. Something big started right here!"

Faneuil Hall looked a little like a school to Stanley. It was three stories tall, and it had a dome peeking up from the top, almost like a chimney. It looked different from all the other buildings around it. Older, and more serious. I bet that's just how it looked in colonial times, Stanley thought.

"I think we should go in!" said Mrs. Lambchop. "Then we can follow

the Freedom Trail from here and see Boston's other historic sites."

"I'm afraid I need to say good-bye for now," said Dr. Dan. "I have some meetings to get to. But I will see you tomorrow! Stanley, I can't wait to hear your speech. It will be a highlight of the conference!"

"Oh, um, sure, see you tomorrow," he said uncomfortably, looking at the ground. Stanley had missed his chance.

Dr. Dan waved good-bye until he disappeared into the crowd. It felt like a hundred butterflies had just landed in Stanley's stomach. Somehow he'd made his big mistake even bigger!

There was nothing left to do except

follow his family through Faneuil Hall. It looked like an old-fashioned auditorium, with rows of wooden chairs facing forward. There were balconies with *more* chairs along the side. There was room for a lot of colonists in here, Stanley thought.

Mrs. Lambchop was holding a brochure. "The grasshopper weather vane on top of this building's cupola is a well-known symbol of the city," she read.

A weather vane was a tool that showed the direction of the wind. Stanley had seen one at the airport. But what in the world was a cupola? Could it be a fancy word for the dome he saw outside? Mrs. Lambchop loved fancy words. Stanley listened, even though he didn't understand much. He didn't want to think about anything else.

Then he heard a voice next to him. "Is that Flat Stanley?"

It reminded Stanley of something important.

Being flat—and being famous—was a part of who he was. And nobody, not even the doctors, was going change that. Because Stanley wouldn't let them!

# Strangers from the Past

When he turned to see who was speaking, Stanley was surprised. They looked like people from another time!

A man was wearing a long gray coat over a pair of short pants. A fancy white collar peeked out of the top of the coat. His shoes were heavy and black, and his hat had three corners. It reminded Stanley of what a pirate might wear.

Next to this man stood a woman in a blue dress that reached all the way to the floor. Her soft white hat was tied under her chin, like a baby's hat. Stanley had never seen a grown-up wearing a bonnet!

"Good afternoon, sir," said the man to Stanley, holding out his hand. "I am Mr. Simon Bradford. And surely you must be Stanley Lambchop."

"How do you know who I am? Aren't you from colonial times?" Stanley wasn't sure if he should shake hands. What if a handshake whisked *him* back in time, too?

The woman in the bonnet smiled. "Have no fear," she said. "I am Hannah

Noble, daughter of a patriot." She lowered her voice to add something. "I am also a local guide."

Oh! Stanley thought. A tour guide, like Beacon Jill! She and the man were only pretending to be people from another time. The bonnet was a costume!

"Nice to meet you," said Stanley politely.

Mr. Simon Bradford smiled. "What brings a fine flat fellow like you to Boston?" he asked.

"We're on a family trip," said Stanley.

"Would you care to join us on a walk through history?" asked Hannah. "We will show you early Boston from a colonist's point of view."

"You will see the sights, hear the sounds, meet the people, and taste the tastes of Boston in the 1700s," said Mr. Bradford. "Just as they really were."

Arthur had stopped taking pictures. He was watching the guides curiously.

Stanley didn't think his brother would want to join another tour. But Arthur surprised him. "Taste the tastes?" he asked.

Hannah Noble turned to him. "Many people don't know that colonists in Boston were fond of chocolate!"

"That is all I need to hear," Arthur said. Next thing Stanley knew, his brother was practically begging to go on the tour! And of course Mr. and Mrs. Lambchop were thrilled. These guides would take them to the next stop on the Freedom Trail: the home of Paul Revere.

"Isn't this perfect?" Mr. Lambchop said. "We'll get an authentic colonial experience! We won't just walk the Freedom Trail. We'll *live* the Freedom Trail."

That sounded better than living the family vacation, Stanley thought glumly. He had really messed things up with Dr. Dan, and he didn't know how to fix them.

The Lambchop family followed Mr.

Bradford and Hannah Noble through the streets of Boston. People stared at their clothing, but the guides acted like they didn't even notice. Hannah swept her skirt up when they crossed the street. Mr. Bradford tipped his hat at a passing bus.

Soon they arrived at a small wooden house. "Here we are," said Hannah. The Lambchops followed the guides inside.

"This house was built in 1680," Hannah said. "It was already old when Paul Revere moved in!" It looked like the house itself had traveled back in time, Stanley thought.

It was cool and dark inside the house. The wooden floor was a little uneven. The hallway was so narrow that only Stanley could walk through easily.

"Paul Revere lived here for many years. This is where he raised his sixteen children and ran his family's silver business. But that's not why we remember him today," said Mr. Bradford.

He cleared his throat. "In the 1700s," he began, "the people of Boston grew tired of living under British rule. The British made the colonists follow laws they didn't like. One law was that they were supposed to buy tea from only one place. When a ship arrived with this tea, angry colonists dumped it all into Boston Harbor! This was known as the Boston Tea Party, and Paul Revere was one of its leaders."

"That's when the colonists started drinking hot cocoa instead of tea!" Mr. Lambchop joked.

Mr. Bradford smiled and continued. "Other colonies were tired of British rule, too. They wanted to know what was happening in Boston. But it wasn't easy for them to be in touch with each other. There were no phones or computers, and letters took a long time to arrive. Sometimes they sent people with the news instead of sending letters.

"I know what that's like!" Stanley

blurted out. Stanley was flat enough to be folded up in an envelope and shipped in a package. "I've done that many times!"

"Well, you're lucky. You can be a person and a letter all at once," Mrs. Lambchop pointed out.

"Paul Revere was often a messenger," said Mr. Bradford. "Sometimes he would ride his horse all the way from Boston to Philadelphia just to share some news. It was a long trip, but he was a fast rider."

Hannah picked up the story from there. "Then one night," she said, "British soldiers arrived in Boston. They were there to make sure the colonists followed the laws. Many colonists were afraid there would be a war."

Mr. Bradford led the Lambchops through another door. "Paul Revere helped spread the word that the soldiers were there. He arranged for two lanterns to be put in the steeple of the Old North Church. That was a code to tell people how the soldiers had arrived. They had not marched into the city. They had come on ships."

"Then Revere set out on his horse," Hannah finished. "He needed to warn his friends Samuel Adams and John Hancock that some of those soldiers were coming to arrest them. Adams and Hancock were in a town called Lexington. Paul Revere had to get to them before the soldiers did!"

She paused for a moment. Stanley couldn't take the suspense.

"Did he get there in time?" asked Stanley.

"Yes and no," Hannah replied.

"What? Do you mean yes? Or no?" Stanley asked again.

She smiled and avoided the question. "Let me show you around this house!"

Now the Lambchops were in a room with a big brick fireplace. Black pots and pans hung over the section where a fire would be. Were they for cooking? Stanley wondered. Was this

the kitchen? It wasn't like his family's
kitchen at all.

Mr. Bradford said, "Paul Revere
was an important figure in American

history.   But his life in Boston was just like that of other colonists. He worked hard and lived simply. His family cooked over a wood fire, right here. They ate in this kitchen in the summer months. In the winter, they ate upstairs where it was warmer."

Stanley frowned. "They didn't have any heat?" he said. "They must have been freezing." Boston got a lot of snow in winter.

Mr. Bradford led the boys to a table where there was a silver teapot and a group of silver cups. "These items are like the ones that Paul Revere made in his shop," he said. "His job was to melt the metal and shape it into things that people could use."

He began to pour from the pot.

"No tea for me," said Arthur. "I mean, no thank you. At least not if it is the British kind."

Hannah laughed. "Luckily, this is hot chocolate, just for you! But I see you are getting into the spirit of our tour. That is why I would like to invite you to a special event. Later this afternoon, we will be re-creating Paul Revere's ride! Would you like to see him carry word to Lexington?"

Stanley wanted to know how this story ended. What happened to Paul

Revere? Did he keep his friends from getting arrested?

Mr. Lambchop looked hopefully at Mrs. Lambchop. "It could be very educational," he pointed out.

"It will be an adventure!" Arthur exclaimed.

Mrs. Lambchop spoke for the whole family. "Of course! We would love to!"

# Secret Mission

At the edge of the Charles River, Stanley and his family waited for Paul Revere to arrive. Or for someone who was dressed up as Paul Revere, anyway. As soon as he got here, their adventure would begin!

It was hard to believe that, just the day before, they had seen this river from a duck boat. Or that Stanley had taken a swim! That seemed like a long time ago now. But not as long ago as the 1700s. Now his family looked like they were from that time themselves.

The Lambchops had changed their clothes and were now dressed like Boston colonists! Mrs. Lambchop was wearing a long dress. The boys and Mr. Lambchop were in short pants and long blue coats. Hannah had told them that the colonists wore blue and the British soldiers wore red. The colonists had a nickname for the British soldiers. They called them redcoats!

Stanley didn't mind the ruffled shirt he was wearing under the coat. He didn't mind the stiff shoes on his

feet. The outfit was so different from his usual clothes that he felt like it was Halloween. The only problem was the hat. No matter what Stanley did, the three-cornered hat would not fit on his two-cornered head. It wobbled all over the place.

Mr. Bradford would be rowing the Lambchops, with Paul Revere, across the river to a different part of the city. Once they arrived, Paul Revere would get on a horse and ride to Lexington. He would try to get there before a group of people pretending to be British soldiers. He would also try to get there before the sun set!

"Here he is!" said Mr. Bradford as

Paul Revere approached.

Paul Revere was tall and strong. He nodded at the Lambchop family, and stepped into Mr. Bradford's rowboat. He kept his head down. It looked like he was hiding.

"Remember," said Mr. Bradford, "Paul Revere took this trip in secret. If anyone spotted him crossing the water, he wouldn't be able to take his ride."

Maybe that was why he didn't say hello, Stanley realized. He didn't want to make any noise. This was a secret mission!

Present-day Boston was still alive around them. Stanley saw sailboats and water taxis on the river. But there was

only open water in front of the simple rowboat.

Stanley pretended he was on a secret mission, too. It made him feel a little nervous, but also excited.

There were six people in the rowboat, and Mr. Bradford worked hard to get it going. "This is going to take forever!" Arthur whispered to his father.

"There were no motorboats in colonial times," his father whispered back. "You just need to be patient."

Mr. Bradford rowed silently across the water. Every time he dipped the paddles, he made sure there was no splash. If there were real British soldiers out here, Stanley was pretty sure no one would hear them.

After a while, Mr. Bradford worked up some speed and they coasted across the water. "That breeze feels nice," said Mrs. Lambchop.

Maybe it was nice for a tired traveler, but it was not that nice for Stanley. He was too flat and too light to withstand it. In the middle of the rowboat, he had nothing to hang onto. Suddenly, with another gust of wind, Stanley was airborne. His legs flew up and his body went upside down!

Mr. Lambchop grabbed his hands just in time. "I've got you!" he cried. "Just hold on."

Stanley was sticking up out of the boat like a sail. He was flapping loudly in the wind. A sail was the last thing he wanted to be.

Stanley hovered above the rowboat. The wind twisted him all around. He imagined everyone on the whole river could see him now. Did they think he was a flag? A kite? A lost sweater? So much for the secret mission.

"Just stay calm!" his mother said. "We're almost there!"

Paul Revere kept his head down and coughed. Up in the air, Stanley turned red. He could tell that Paul Revere wasn't happy about all this noise.

Then Mr. Bradford stopped rowing

for a moment, and the breeze died down. Stanley almost belly-flopped into the water before his father caught him.

Stanley sat in the boat. He tried to catch his breath. Then Arthur hopped onto his lap! "I'll weigh you down," Arthur explained.

His little brother wasn't the only thing weighing him down as they proceeded across the water. His thoughts were heavy, too. Stanley was embarrassed that he'd almost ruined the mission. And he was sad because his three-cornered hat was gone! It had been hard to wear, but now Stanley missed it. He didn't look like a colonist anymore. He just looked like a kid in a funny outfit. He looked into the water and imagined his hat going out to sea.

Ahead of them was the neighborhood of Charlestown, where Paul Revere's horse would be waiting. Behind them was the Boston skyline. Mrs. Lambchop turned to look. She tapped Stanley on the shoulder and pointed at a church steeple in the distance. "It's the Old North Church!" she said in a low voice, full of wonder. "There are the signals!"

Paul Revere had arranged for two lanterns to be hung there—just for a minute—the night of his ride. The signals told the people of Boston that the British soldiers had arrived on ships. Someone had even written a

famous poem about it. Mrs. Lambchop
knew the poem by heart! She said some
of the lines out loud, until Stanley saw
the lights blink off.

"*He said to his friend, "If the British
march
By land or sea from the town to-night
Hang a lantern aloft in the belfry
arch*

*Of the North Church tower as a*
*signal light, —*
*One, if by land, and two, if by sea;*
*And I on the opposite shore will*
*be . . ."'"*

Soon Mr. Bradford reached the other side of the river. He held the rowboat steady as the passengers climbed out, one by one.

In the shadows, Stanley could see another man dressed as a colonist. He shook Paul Revere's hand and gave him a horse's reins. The horse sneezed, and Mr. Revere laughed.

Maybe he was more friendly than

he looked, Stanley thought. Maybe he was less worried about staying hidden, now that they were off the river. Even if British soldiers spotted him, Revere could outrun them. He could ride like the wind!

Just then, Paul Revere stepped out of the shadows, looked at the Lambchops, and finally spoke. "You must be Flat Stanley."

"Yes . . . I am . . . ," he stammered. He couldn't believe it. Even Paul Revere knew who he was! It did make him feel a little better.

Mr. Revere smiled. "Would you like to go for a ride?"

He turned to Mr. and Mrs. Lambchop. "May I take Stanley to Lexington with me? It will be a ride he'll never forget!"

Stanley answered without even thinking. "I love to deliver messages!" he said.

Mr. Lambchop chimed in right away. "Of course! Stanley won't just see the ride of Paul Revere. He'll *live* the ride of Paul Revere!"

This was the flip side of being flat, Stanley realized. Sometimes he needed special treatment, like when he was in danger of blowing away. But he also got to do special things! His stomach was full of butterflies again, but this time he was only excited, not afraid. He threw one flat leg over the horse and hung on tight.

Then Mr. Revere handed him something. It had three corners. It was a little damp around the edges. But Stanley knew just what it was. Somehow Paul Revere had saved it.

They made plans to meet up with Stanley's family in Lexington. Then Mr. Revere climbed onto the horse, too. And as they rode away, he yelled, "We're off, Stanley! Hold on to your hat!"

# "Midnight" Ride

The road was a blur to Stanley. He could barely tell that they were leaving the city and heading into the smaller towns around Boston. The buildings were shorter here, and there was a lot less traffic. But Stanley couldn't see the people on the sidewalks, or the names of the stores they passed. Paul Revere was riding too fast!

They were racing the British to warn some of the colonists' most important leaders. But would they get to Lexington in time? Or would Samuel Adams and John Hancock be arrested before they got there?

Stanley squirmed in the saddle behind Mr. Revere. He held on tight—one hand around Paul Revere, the other on his hat—as the horse flew past cars and bicycles. Its hooves pounded so loudly that Stanley couldn't hear anything else.

He could see the moon now, peeking out from behind some clouds. Soon it would be dark, and maybe rainy. Was this what it was like on the night the real Paul Revere rode to Lexington? What was the real Paul Revere thinking as he rushed along the road? Stanley wondered. Behind every shadow, and around every corner, there could have been someone waiting to stop him.

The horse was running down a twisty road. He veered right, and Stanley leaned into the turn. But when the horse veered left, Stanley was too late.

Suddenly, it was like the rowboat all over again! One minute, he was on the horse; the next minute, he was carried away by a gust of wind. Stanley drifted

behind the horse like a boy-shaped leaf, and Mr. Revere didn't hear or feel a thing. Even when Stanley yelled, "Help! HELP!"

Stanley floated to the ground like a piece of paper, just before the horse and rider disappeared around a bend in the road. He could hear the pounding hooves for a while longer . . . then nothing.

Stanley got out of the street quickly. His arm felt a little bruised from where'd he'd fallen, but his feelings were bruised, too. In just a few seconds, he'd gone from the center of American history to the side of the road.

Stanley had no idea what to do. He

couldn't get in touch with Mr. Revere. He couldn't get in touch with his family. He didn't even know where he was! Even speaking at a conference of doctors with Dr. Dan would be better than this.

Then he remembered Paul Revere. Not the one who'd dropped him, but the real one.

He was probably scared as he raced for Lexington, right? He must have been incredibly brave.

Stanley would have to be brave, too, if he was ever going to find his way out of here. He'd have to be strong. And if he could find some courage right now, maybe he could also find the courage to talk to Dr. Dan. In spite of the problems it caused for him, Stanley still hadn't changed his mind about staying flat forever.

Stanley stood up, brushed himself off, and started walking.

It was so quiet in this neighborhood, wherever it was, that he could hear

each of his footsteps clearly. As each one echoed, Stanley had a new thought.

He could reach his parents, if only he could find a phone.

In the twenty-first century, Lexington was probably full of phones!

Once he reached his parents, they would rescue him.

He would be safe.

But . . . to find a phone, he would have to ask someone.

He would have to talk to strangers.

How would he begin?

Stanley's mind jumped to the real Paul Revere again. As he rode to Lexington, he spread the word that the British army was on its way. After all, Samuel Adams and John Hancock weren't the only people who needed to know that an army had landed in Boston. Without his news, the army could have launched a surprise attack.

Stanley was dressed as a colonist. Anyone could guess that he was part of a reenactment. If he spoke to people as a colonist, they would be curious, for sure!

It was the strangest way ever to start a conversation, but Stanley would give it a try.

He passed a row of houses with green lawns. The first person he saw was mowing the grass. "The British are coming!" Stanley told him.

The man just pointed to his headphones. He couldn't hear what Stanley was saying.

Stanley walked a little faster. He called up to a family eating dinner outside on their porch. "The British are coming!" They waved at him and smiled, like he had just made a polite remark about the weather. When the real Paul Revere rode, this news would have been like a lightning bolt!

A bicycle passed, and Stanley said it again. "The British are coming! Get ready!" The cyclist turned around and just stared as he rode by.

I must look a little funny, Stanley

thought. Maybe I should try something else.

He could see a boy walking toward him, just about his age. He was taking a dog for a walk. When the dog spotted Stanley, he pulled at the end of his leash. Stanley stopped to pet him. "The British are coming," he told the dog. He felt a little funny telling the boy.

But the boy, unlike the other people, seemed to understand. "Are you part of a reenactment?" he asked. "We have them a lot here in Lexington."

Now Stanley knew where he was, at least.

The boy walked around Stanley, looking him up and down. "Are you pretending to be a British colonist, though? Or pretending to be Flat Stanley?"

Stanley smiled. "Both, actually." It took him a while to explain. He had never been so happy to be famous.

The boy smiled back. "I'm Ryan Rogers," he said. "Why don't you come to my house? You can call your parents, and you can wait there until they come to get you."

On the way, he asked Stanley about all of his adventures. He seemed to know every place Flat Stanley had ever been!

Stanley followed Ryan to his house. Arthur would love this place! he thought. In every room, there was some kind of Red Sox memorabilia. There were signed photos on the walls. There were pennants in the windows. There was a book of rare baseball cards on the coffee table. When Ryan offered Stanley some water, it came in a cup that looked like a baseball!

"Here's the phone," said Ryan,

handing it to Stanley. "My dad said we can drive you to meet your family, once you find out where they are."

While he waited for his parents to answer the phone, Stanley looked around Ryan's living room. There were rows of trophies on shelves. In a glass case, he saw a battered glove, a Red Sox jersey, and a gleaming golden ring. It looked like a ring you would have if you were part of a winning team.

"Someone here really loves the Red Sox," Stanley said to Ryan.

Just then, Mrs. Lambchop answered the phone. "Hi, Mom," said Stanley. "Don't worry—I am fine. But I flew off

Mr. Revere's horse . . ." He tried not to sound upset.

"I am so happy to hear your voice!" said Mrs. Lambchop. "We were so worried when Mr. Revere arrived without you!"

"So he got there?" Stanley asked urgently. "Did he warn Samuel Adams and John Hancock?"

"Mr. Revere made it safe and sound," Mrs. Lambchop reported. "He has continued on to Concord, where the colonists have stored their weapons."

Stanley knew what would happen next. Any minute now, colonists would exchange fire with the British army on the Lexington town green. The Revolutionary War was about to begin! Thanks to Paul Revere, some of the colonists' most important leaders were safe!

"Stay right where you are," his mother said. "We will be there any minute to pick you up."

"Oh," said Stanley. "You don't need to pick me up. A boy named Ryan rescued me. His father will drive me to meet you on the town green."

Mrs. Lambchop was careful with people she didn't know. "Does Ryan have a nice family?" she asked nervously.

But Stanley knew he would be safe. "Don't worry, Mom," he said. "Ryan's dad is not a stranger. He knows a lot about us, because we are the Lambchops. But we know a lot about him, too. He is the left fielder for the Boston Red Sox!"

# Fenway Park

Finally, the Lambchops were doing what Arthur wanted to do. They were finished with making history. The next day, they went to a baseball game! They were the guests of Ryan Rogers and his father, Richie Rogers, at Boston's Fenway Park.

As Stanley walked through the entrance of the baseball field, it felt like he was going back in time all over again. Fenway Park was more than a hundred years old!

Stanley and Arthur followed Ryan onto the field. The Red Sox were practicing! They were doing what all baseball players—even kids—did before games. They were throwing, catching, and hitting. The difference was that the throws, catches, and hits went much farther than any that Stanley had ever seen. He watched one of the Red Sox hit a ball right out of the park!

"That's just a practice hit?" Arthur asked in amazement.

Ryan grinned. "Right over the Green Monster!" he said.

"What do you mean?" Stanley asked. He did not see any monsters on the field. Ryan pointed at the place where the ball had disappeared. There was a tall green wall, stretching across left field. "See right there? That's the Green Monster! It is thirty-seven feet tall."

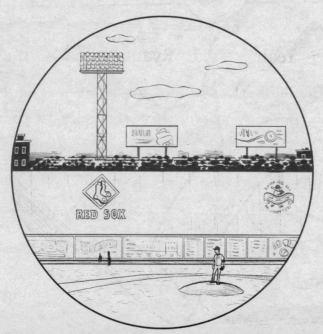

"It's really hard to hit the ball over it, right?" Arthur said.

Ryan frowned. "Well, usually. But today we're playing the Yankees, and anything is possible. Do you know about Zane Wayne?"

"I've heard he can hit any spot he aims for," Arthur said. "He is super strong, and he has great control of the ball."

"Yeah," said Ryan. "That's the problem."

Just then, a player jogged up to the boys. "Is that Arthur Lambchop?" he asked, ruffling Arthur's hair. Arthur knew a lot about the Red Sox, but he didn't expect the Red Sox to know anything about him! But this was Ryan's father, Richie Rogers. In the car, Stanley had told him all about his brother.

"I'm so glad you're here for this big game," Richie said to Arthur, signing a baseball.

Stanley didn't know why the game was important, but Arthur did. "If you win today, you'll be in first place in the league, right?" he said.

Richie Rogers gave Arthur a high-five. "I hear you're our number one fan," he said. "That's why I've reserved top-notch seats for your family. Right on top of the Green Monster!"

Sure enough, the seats were right at the edge of the wall. From here, Stanley could see everything except the old-fashioned scoreboard, which was on the wall below him. He even saw an old friend! Zoey, from the duck tour, was sitting two rows behind them. She waved shyly at the boys. She showed them that she still had her ducky!

"I think Lucky is cheering for the Red Sox, too," said Arthur.

As the game began and the Red Sox pitcher approached the mound, Ryan said, "We have our best pitcher out there. I just hope he can keep the Yankees from hitting. Zane Wayne could do some serious damage."

The first pitch was in the air. "Ball one!"

"Zane Wayne does strike out sometimes," Arthur pointed out.

"I know," said Ryan. "But we have a big weak spot tonight, and we don't know if he knows about it."

"What is it?" Stanley asked.

"Problems with hitting? Or fielding? Or both?"

Ryan lowered his voice and leaned toward the boys. "Actually, neither. The problem is that there's a hole in the Green Monster. If Zane Wayne sees it, he can hit a ball right at it. And if it goes through, he'll have a home run!"

Stanley thought for a minute. Ryan had helped him in Lexington. Could he help Ryan at Fenway Park?

"I have an idea," Stanley said when the first half of the inning ended. "But we have to be fast. Zane Wayne is the next Yankee at bat!"

Stanley told his parents that they

were going to get some snacks. While Arthur and Ryan stood in line for food, though, Stanley went to the gift shop. He bought himself a T-shirt that was the same color as the Green Monster! Quickly, he slipped it on. He also slipped two pieces of bubble gum into his mouth.

He found the other boys paying for a hot dog and a big bag of popcorn. As they carried their snacks through the crowd, Stanley spotted yet another familiar face. It was Dr. Dan! He was taking in a game before the conference ended tonight with his speech—and Stanley's. For now, Stanley ducked out of sight, but he would make sure to find Dr. Dan after the game. Stanley was ready to be as brave as Paul Revere.

The boys were back at their seats before the inning ended. Stanley took a deep breath. "Here's what I'm going to do," he told the boys. "I'm going to cover the hole!"

"But how will you get to it?" Arthur asked. "It's in the middle of the wall!"

"Easy!" said Ryan. "There's a ladder that leads right there. What a great idea!"

"And you'll . . . stick to the wall?" Arthur said. "How is that going to work?"

Stanley blew a big, sticky bubble. "The gum should hold me for Zane Wayne's at bat," he said. "And I will be so flat and so green that I'll blend right in!"

When the announcer called Zane Wayne's name, there were a few cheers and a few boos. He was not very popular at Fenway Park. While the whole crowd's attention was on the Yankees star, Stanley crept down the ladder in his green shirt.

He spotted the hole right away and covered it with his belly. With gum on his hands and feet, he was suspended on the wall at four points. It was not very comfortable, Stanley had to admit.

But nobody could see his face. And nobody could see the hole.

The only problem was that *he* couldn't see anything, either. He didn't know what Zane Wayne was doing. He imagined the slugger swaggering toward the plate. He imagined him taking a practice swing. But did he know where to aim? Stanley wondered. He was about to find out!

"Strike one!" the announcer said. There was some applause for the pitcher.

A second later, though, the announcer said, "Ball one. Ball two!"

The pitches were coming quickly, and

Zane Wayne knew just how to handle them. He probably knew what to expect from this pitcher, Stanley thought. But did he know about the hole in the wall?

Just then, he heard a sharp crack. It might have been a thunderbolt. Or it might have been the sound of Zane Wayne's bat whacking the ball.

Suddenly, the crowd was silent, like it was waiting. There was a chorus of "Oh no!" from the section above the Green Monster. The ball had to be coming toward the outfield!

Stanley pressed himself against the hole in the wall. He braced for a shock. Then he felt a sharp gust of wind, like a tiny rocket had passed him by. There was another crack, just above his shoulder, where the ball hit.

Yes, Zane Wayne knew about the hole. But he had missed it by two inches, and there was no way it could bounce in by mistake.

Flat Stanley had it covered.

And Zane Wayne was out!

For his next at bat, Stanley did a repeat performance. And by the time Zane Wayne was up again, in the eighth inning, he was replaced by a pinch hitter.

Arthur could see him in the Yankees dugout. "He doesn't look very happy," he reported.

But Stanley was happier than he had been on the whole Boston trip. He knew what he had to do, and now he had the courage to do it.

When the game was over, the score was 1-0, Red Sox. One home run from

Zane Wayne would have made a big difference. "We couldn't have done it without you, Stanley!" Ryan said, jumping out of his seat. "You saved the game!"

The boys gathered their things. They followed Mr. and Mrs. Lambchop out of the stadium. "There's someone I need to talk to," Stanley told his brother and Ryan. "Dr. Dan is around here, somewhere. I have something important to tell him."

Ryan Rogers showed Stanley where to wait. "This is the busiest exit," he explained. "I am sure it's where your friend will walk out. And you are welcome at Fenway Park any time!"

While Arthur and his parents went back to the gift shop, Stanley stood near the exit. The crowds thinned out until there were only a few baseball fans left, and many of them stared curiously at Stanley. He didn't even care. He was *proud* to be flat! He was just about to give up when Dr. Dan walked by.

"Stanley Lambchop," he said in surprise. "Shouldn't you be getting ready for your big night?"

Stanley still hated to let him down. But he couldn't let himself down, either!

This time, he got right to his point. "Dr. Dan," he said, "I can't give a speech tonight!"

"Oh no!" he said. Dr. Dan looked just

the way he did back home in his office. He looked worried about Stanley! "Are you feeling all right? Are you hurt?"

Stanley laughed. "No . . . nothing like that! I'm fine! It's just that . . . I don't want to talk about the way your research could help me. Even though it sounds amazing," he added quickly. "I'm sure you'll help tons of people someday.

But . . . I don't think I need any help myself, thanks." He was pretty sure he was turning red with embarrassment! But at least he had spoken up. At last!

For some reason, Dr. Dan was smiling. "Was that you, on the Green Monster? Covering the hole?" he asked.

Stanley's eyes widened. "How did you know about that? Did you see me?"

"I have my ways," said Dr. Dan. "And I have many friends in Boston, including a famous player named Richie Rogers."

Stanley's jaw dropped. "You know him?" he asked.

Dr. Dan said, "Yes, I know him well.

Just like I know you. And I would never want either of you to change, unless you wanted to."

Judging from his house, Stanley was pretty sure Richie Rogers loved being part of the Red Sox. He probably didn't want to change his life any more than Stanley did.

Dr. Dan continued, "The whole point of the research is to give people a choice. If they want to lose weight, or gain weight, they will be able to do it. But people who want to stay the way they are, should stay the way are. People who are flat should stay flat!"

Stanley let out a long breath. Dr. Dan understood what he was worried about.

What a relief! But that wasn't the *only* thing he was worried about.

"Thanks, Dr. Dan!" said Stanley. "I feel so much better now! But what about Dr. Deb? What about the speech? The doctors at the conference are expecting me!"

"Well, maybe you could talk about something else," said Dr. Dan.

"Like what?" said Stanley. What else would anyone want to hear from a flat boy?

Dr. Dan rubbed his chin thoughtfully for a second. Then his eyes lit up.

"There may be people in the audience who would like to be flat themselves, someday. That is probably a long way off," Dr. Dan admitted. "But could you tell them some of the amazing things you get to do *because* you are flat?"

Stanley thought about being a life preserver. He thought about traveling back in time—sort of—and riding with Paul Revere. He thought about saving the game for the Red Sox. Maybe someday other people would get to have adventures like these, too.

Stanley grinned at Dr. Dan. He would do the speech, he decided. But now he had one more question.

"How much time would I get?" Stanley asked Dr. Dan. "Because I have a *lot* to say!"

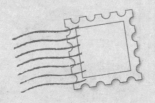

# WHAT YOU NEED TO KNOW ABOUT BOSTON AND PAUL REVERE!

The John Hancock Tower is officially named 200 Clarendon, but everyone still calls it the John Hancock Tower. The building is sixty stories tall and contains thirteen acres of glass!

There are colored lights on the top of the John Hancock Tower that show the weather:
"Steady blue, clear view.
Flashing blue, clouds due.
Steady red, rain ahead.
Flashing red, snow instead."

The oldest public park in the United States is the Boston Common. It dates back to 1634.

Fenway Park is the oldest original Major League Baseball stadium still in use. It opened in 1912.

The Green Monster of Fenway Park is the thirty-seven-foot-high wall located beyond left field. It's named after the green paint color that covers the wall.

Boston is the home of North America's first college, Harvard University, which was founded in 1636.

In 1716, the first American lighthouse was built on a small island in Boston Harbor.

On March 18, 1990, the largest art theft in the history of the United States happened in Boston. The stolen paintings have never been recovered.

Originally, the town of Boston was named Shawmut. But on September 17, 1630, colonists renamed it Boston, after a town in England called Boston.

The Red Sox were named in 1907 by their owner at the time, John I. Taylor. Before that, they had many different names, including the Americans, the Pilgrims, the Somersets, the Puritans, and the Plymouth Rocks.

On top of the gold dome of the State House in Boston sits a golden pinecone.

Paul Revere's ride to warn the colonists of the British became famous because of an 1861 Henry Wadsworth Longfellow poem. But the poem got several facts wrong!

The horse that Paul Revere rode on the night of April 18, 1775, was borrowed from a merchant named John Larkin. The horse was a mare named Brown Beauty.

Many people say that as he rode to warn the colonists, Paul Revere shouted out "the British are coming!" But he never actually said this!

In addition to being a silversmith and artist, Paul Revere was also the leader of a group of colonists that spied on British soldiers.

Boston Duck tours have been around since October 4th, 1994, when they had four duck boats. Now, they have twenty-eight boats!

A bronze statue in Boston's Public Garden commemorates a famous children's book called *Make Way for Ducklings*. The story is about a pair of mallards who decide to raise their ducklings on an island in the garden.

Since 1742, Faneuil Hall has been both a marketplace and a meeting hall. It was destroyed by fire in 1761, and only the brick walls survived. In 1762 the colonists had it rebuilt, and in 1775, when the British were occupying Boston, it was used as a theater.

The Ted Williams Tunnel is ninety feet below the surface of Boston Harbor, making it the deepest tunnel in North America.

The Boston Cream Pie is the official state dessert of Massachusetts. It was invented at the Omni Parker House.